Corte Madera
E Hamilton
Hamilton, K. R. (Kersten
R.)
Red truck
31111028173241   7/68

ZOOOOM!

ZOOOOM!

ZC

ZO

ZOOOOM!

For Benja, who's truckin' with Jesus—KH

To Rio—
Pallina and Patrick's artwork—VP

VIKING
Published by Penguin Group
Penguin Young Readers Group, 345 Hudson Street, New York, New York 10014, U.S.A.
Penguin Group (Canada), 90 Eglinton Avenue East, Suite 700, Toronto, Ontario, Canada M4P 2Y3
(a division of Pearson Penguin Canada Inc.)

Penguin Books Ltd, Registered Offices: 80 Strand, London WC2R ORL, England

First published in 2008 by Viking, a division of Penguin Young Readers Group

1   3   5   7   9   10   8   6   4   2

LIBRARY OF CONGRESS CATALOGING-IN-PUBLICATION DATA
Hamilton, K. R. (Kersten R.)
Red truck / by Kersten Hamilton ; illustrated by Valeria Petrone.
p. cm.
Summary: When a school bus gets stuck in the mud, Red Truck the tow truck saves the day by pulling it out.
ISBN 978-0-670-06275-1 (hardcover)
[1. Wreckers (Vehicles)—Fiction. 2. Trucks—Fiction. 3. Stories in rhyme.] I. Petrone, Valeria, ill. II. Title.
PZ8.3.H1853Re 2008
[E]—dc22
2007022902

Manufactured in China
Set in Circus Mouse Book Medium
Book design by Jim Hoover

RED TRUCK

by **Kersten Hamilton**
illustrated by **Valeria Petrone**

VIKING

RED TRUCK
is a tow truck,
a work truck,
not a show
truck.

Can

Red Truck

make it

UP

the hill?

Red Truck **CAN!**
Red Truck **WILL!**

Other trucks can't
cross the mud.

Red Truck tried
Red Truck **COULD.**

SPLOOOOSH!

Slipping, sliding
down the slope.
"Red Truck is our
only hope."

HURRY, RED TRUCK!

Hooks are on,
chains are tight—
PULL, Red Truck,
with all your
MIGHT!

School Bus

PULLLL!

Splishy-splashy wet HOORAY!

Our hero for a rainy day . . .

is RED TRUCK!